Faith Healer

Trevor Millum

Folens

© 2004 Folens Limited, on behalf of the author.

United Kingdom: Folens Publishers, Apex Business Centre, Boscombe
Road, Dunstable, LU5 4RL.
Email: folens@folens.com

Ireland: Folens Publishers, Greenhills Road, Tallaght, Dublin 24.
Email: info@folens.ie

Poland: JUKA, ul. Renesansowa 38, Warsaw 01-905.

Editor: Kay Macmullan
Layout artist: Suzanne Ward
Cover design: John Hawkins

First published 2004 by Folens Limited.

British Library Cataloguing in Publication Data. A catalogue record for
this publication is available from the British Library.

ISBN 1 84303 727–0

Contents

1   The girl on the road   5

2   Accident black spot   14

3   Truck stop   19

4   Delivered   25

5   A call for help   32

6   Errand of mercy   38

7   Waiting for a miracle   45

8   Back to reality   52

9   Out of the blue   56

The story so far

If you haven't read an *On the edge* book before:
The stories take place in and around a row of shops and buildings called Pier Parade in Brightsea, right next to the sea. There's Big Fry, the fish and chip shop; Drop Zone, the drop-in centre for local teenagers; Macmillan's, the sweet and souvenir shop; Anglers' Haven, the fishing tackle shop; the Surf 'n' Skate shop and, of course, the Brightsea Beach Bar (the 3Bs).

If you have read an *On the edge* book you may have met some of these people before.

Roy Macmillan:	*a long-distance lorry driver.*
Susan Macmillan:	*runs Macmillan's, the sweet and souvenir shop in Pier Parade.*
Jan Macmillan:	*their daughter.*

So, what's been going on?
Long-distance lorry driver Roy's short temper and tiredness cause him to have a serious car crash in which he almost loses his life. Fortunately, he pulls through, but the incident shakes him up badly, and he is trying to drive more carefully – and keep his cool – especially for his children's sake.

What happens in this story?
Roy's on a long run when he picks up a young woman hitching. She is on her way to see a faith healer, hoping he can help her wheelchair-bound father recover from a bad accident. Roy feels sorry for her and her family, but surely this sort of thing can't really work, can it?

4

1

The girl on the road

Roy Macmillan climbed into the cab and started the engine.

He checked the delivery addresses and his timesheet.

He nodded to himself.

It was a familiar run.

A series of A-roads and then the motorway.

He might be lucky and miss the usual snarl-up around junction 17.

If not – too bad.

In the past, Roy would get upset when there was a hold-up.

Not any more.
Not since he had nearly killed himself –
and several others – some months before.
In wet weather he could feel the metal
plate in his shoulder.
It was a reminder.

As he left the town he passed a couple of
hitch-hikers.
He didn't even pause.
Did they know nothing?
He was pulling up a slope and it was no
place to stop.
Anyway, he wasn't in the mood.

He joined the new by-pass just as the row
of huge yellow lights came on.
He switched his own lights on.
And it was then that he saw the girl on
the side of the road.

She held out her thumb but she didn't
look very hopeful.
On the spur of the moment, he decided
to stop.
Something he never used to do.
But since the accident… well, it had
changed him.

He often stopped now.
He didn't quite know why.
But he thought of Jan, his own daughter.
He recalled the time she'd run off.
This was someone's daughter, too.
Perhaps this girl was trying to get home
before dark.

He leant over and opened the door.
It hung open and he waited.
A hand appeared, grasping the handle,
then a head.
Her other hand grasped a small rucksack.

She was a bit older than Jan, maybe
15 or 16.
Too young to be out hitching – but any
age was too young if you were female.
He had given up telling hitch-hikers that
they shouldn't be doing it.
It was asking for trouble.

She gave him half a smile and plonked
herself down in the seat.
"Thanks," was all she said.

He nodded to her, checked his mirrors
and moved off.
'Not going to be much chat with this one,'
he thought.

He looked sideways at her.
She sat hunched on the seat, her bag on
the floor in front of her – trapped by her
feet.

Feet that were encased in heavy brown boots.
Boots laced with white laces tipped with brass ends.

She stared out from the mess of her collar and her rumpled clothes towards the road.
The road unfolded in front of them.

They both looked ahead.
Yet he sensed she saw only what was behind.
Her eyes – he guessed, because he couldn't see them – were looking inside.
Her hair, lank and black, could have been pretty.
But it hung down, uncombed and unloved.

He thought of Jan and the different ways she could look.

He felt a pang of guilt.

He shouldn't be doing this job, away from home.

He should be back there, with Jan, and with his wife, Susan, and Becky, his younger daughter.

"Going far?" he asked.

This was a question every hitch-hiker had to answer.

Yet she delayed.

He drove on.

Steering wheel in one hand, other hand on the gear lever: that was how he felt most comfortable.

Often his shoulder ached – but he wasn't going to give in.

In the end, the girl spoke.

"Marston," she said. "If you're going that way."

"No avoiding it," he said, though there was.

A silence.

"What's there?" he asked.

"Accident black spot," she replied.

'Christ,' he thought. 'A nutter. Just my luck. Do a good turn and pick up a nutter. I mean, who wants to see accident black spots? It's not like train-spotting, is it?'

He kept these thoughts to himself.

The truck roared on.
The noise was nothing to him.
To her, it was a cover, which meant there was no need to speak.

"Why Marston?" he asked in the end.
"Plenty of accident black spots. Why that one?"
He was curious – not just for an answer but to know if she was sane or not.

The road rumbled beneath them.
The engine was calm and untroubled.

"My dad," she said suddenly. "He was in an accident there."

Roy sighed.
Trust him to put his foot in it.
But she didn't have to tell him.
She could have lied.
'Besides,' he thought, 'at least that makes some sense. She wants to go back to the scene. I can understand that.'

"What happened?" he asked.

"A lorry. Like this one. It hit his car. I don't know – maybe he pulled out too soon…"

Words she had heard but didn't understand.
Pulled out into… the path of a heavy goods vehicle.
No chance.

"You want to see the place?"

She just nodded.

They drove on.
The noise of the engine was like
background music.
Her eyes looked inside.
He kept his own eyes on the road ahead.

2

Accident black spot

He slowed.

The crossroads was coming up.

Another half mile along the road and they'd be there.

It was a vicious crossing.

The sign saying 'accident black spot' just seemed to celebrate its awful history.

He slowed even more.

A car behind him flashed its lights.

In the past he would have shouted at the driver.

Now he just muttered under his breath.

He indicated left.

The car overtook.

The truck came to a halt on the verge.

"You want to get down?" he asked.

She sat still.
Her hair was a curtain.

"Yeah," she said. "I suppose so."

She opened the door and climbed –
almost fell – down.
There was nothing to see.
Just grass verge and a scrubby hedge and,
in the distance, lampposts and the next
set of road signs.

He sat in the cab and watched her.
She walked to the side of the road and
looked up and down the two roads.
It was quiet at this time of day.

Then the lights of a line of cars came into sight, got closer, passed them and disappeared over the hill.
She was lit up like an actress and then forgotten.

He could see how it had happened.
He knew of similar accidents.

So he waited – even though time was ticking by and there were questions in his head.
There were no flowers by the side of the road.
So the girl's father must be still alive…

She came back to the truck.
She heaved herself into the cab and sat back on the well-worn seat.

"Where now?" he asked.

"Going anywhere near Rudston?"

"Could do," he replied. "Why?"

"Someone there I want to see."

He put the truck into gear and pulled out.
Two miles down the road, he said,
"It's getting late. You shouldn't be out on
your own. What are you going to do?"

Her lips tightened.
Her skin was almost transparent in the
yellow light of the street lamps.
"Dunno," she said.

He sighed to himself.
'One good turn just gets you into bother,'
he thought.

"Look," he said, "Rudston is 50 miles
off. I can be there in less than an hour.
But then I stop. I don't drive through the
night. What are your plans? Come on,
you're in my rig now!"

He wasn't prepared for her response.

"I don't have any plans!"

Her carefully composed self broke into pieces.

"I saw the place my dad was hit. Now I need to go to Thomas's. To Thomas's. The healer. He can help him. He can save him."

Tears ran down her cheeks and her words became impossible to hear.

3

Truck stop

Roy pulled in at the next truck stop.
The lorry park was badly surfaced and
there were big puddles everywhere.
In the middle of this wasteland was a low
brick building.
This was Kate's Kaff.
The jolly name of the café always made
him shake his head.
The owner was a big man called Ron who
rarely smiled.
He had never seen any Kate.
But it was clean and it was handy.

"Come on," he said. "We need a cup of
tea."
He knew he had to tell, not ask.

She didn't resist.

She climbed down and followed him to the doorway.

Inside, he guided her to a table in the corner.

He went to the counter and bought two teas and some chocolate.

He kept his eye on her all the time.

He nodded at some of the drivers as he walked back to the table.

They nodded back.

One or two looked at him oddly.

One winked.

"Not what you're thinking, mate," he muttered.

He put the tea in front of her.

"Sugar?" he asked.

She shook her head.

He put sugar in his own tea and placed the chocolate in front of her.
He didn't expect her to eat it.

"Now, tell me what this is all about." he said.

She had stopped sobbing and sniffing.
He was grateful for that.

She sipped some tea.
He waited.

"Why?" she asked.

"Look," he said. "Let's not mess about.
We can drive to Rudston or we can stop at the next police station and you can be in the next squad car home."

She glanced up at him.
"No!" she said. "Don't do that!"

The look on her face made him soften.

"I've got a daughter," he said. "I like to know where she is and what she's up to. Does anyone know where you are? Does anyone know what you're doing?"

She shook her head.

"Right then. Tell me the story."

She sipped more tea.

"I'm trying to help my dad. No one else can. He had this accident and now he's in a wheelchair. They say he'll never be able to walk again. But I found out about this place. A place near Rudston where there's a man who heals people. He's called Thomas. I can't remember his other name."

"You think this man can cure your dad? Can make him walk again?"

"Why not? He's cured all sorts of people. But no one will ask him to cure my dad. So I will."

She sounded defiant.
Her eyes were bright and full of tears.

"OK, OK," said Roy. "I've known stranger things, I s'pose. You got the address?"

"You gonna take me there?"
She looked grateful.

He sighed.
"I might. Well, I'm not going to abandon you in the middle of a strange town. Not now."

She surprised him by opening the chocolate.

"You got a mum?" he asked.

"Yeah," she said. "She does her best."

"Won't she be worried about you?"

"It's her night out. She goes out with her workmates. Our neighbour pops in to see if Dad's all right. It's Mum's one bit of fun. She'll come in and go straight to bed."

She paused.

"I'll call her in the morning if I'm not back."

"Your mum's having a bad time?" he asked, more gently.

He couldn't help thinking about Susan and what it must have been like for her when he was lying in hospital.

"Yeah. We all are. That's the worst thing. My dad – he's not the same. He was cheerful and… well, just normal. Now he's so down all the time. Sometimes he says he wants…"

"What?"

"He wants to die."

The tears started to roll down her cheeks.

4

Delivered

Roy nodded.

"People change when that kind of thing happens to them."

He almost told her about his own accident.

Then he stopped.

She didn't want to be bothered with his stupid story.

He wished he could forget it himself.

"And another thing," he said. "I bet this Thomas doesn't do his healing for free."

"I brought my savings," she said.

"Hang on to them," he said. "You want to help your dad? Don't part with any money till you need to."

She nodded.
"Shouldn't we be going?" she asked.
She pushed the cup away and started to stand up.

Roy looked at her.
She sat down again.

"When I'm ready, miss. Just one more thing. What's your name?"

"Chloe. Chloe Hammond."

"You got a mobile phone?"

She looked surprised.
"Yeah. Why?"

"Can I see it?"

She reached for her bag, found the phone and handed it to him.

"It's switched off," Roy said.

"I didn't want anyone calling me just now."

"Just switch it on for me for a minute."

She did as he asked.
He took it from her and tapped in a number.
A few seconds passed and the phone in Roy's pocket gave a series of beeps.
He took it out and added the caller's number to his address book.
He saved his own number on her phone and handed it back.
Jan had taught him all this while he'd been recovering at home after his accident.
Before then, he hadn't known one end of a mobile from the other.

"I'm Roy," he said gruffly. "Just in case you need it."

He stood up.
"Let's go and find this Thomas," he said.

She had the details written down.
'This kid is organised,' thought Roy.

It was a farm – or what used to be a farm.
Roy had seen signs to it off the main road.
He had never taken much notice.
Rudston Manor Farm – it wasn't
especially unusual.

He swung the lorry down the farm lane.
Experience told him that there would be
somewhere to turn round.
The headlights picked out hedges and
puddles.
He drove slowly.
Finally, they came to a group of buildings.
There were lights in the downstairs
windows.

Another sign said 'Rudston Healing
Centre' and pointed to the right.
The main farm lane went straight on.

He stopped the truck.

"This must be it. I'm not going to drive in there – I might never get out. I'm going on down the lane till I see somewhere to turn round. I'll drop you here."

Suddenly she looked scared.

"Just go and tell them what you told me," he said. "They won't throw you out. And give your mum a call. She can come and get you."

She got down without another word.
He saw her walking towards the main building.
Then she disappeared.

He put the lorry into gear and moved off.

'Poor kid,' he thought. 'Fat chance this Thomas will make her dad walk again. Ah well, not my problem any more. I've done my bit.'

He found a turning place half a mile down the lane.
It was a stockyard that seemed to be part of a working farm.
There was no one about and he turned easily.
He drove slowly back towards the main road.
As he approached the entrance to Rudston Healing Centre, he saw her.
She waved him down.
He swore to himself.
She came round to the driver's side and he leant out of the window.

"It's all right," she said. "They were shut, really, but…"

"But they didn't have much choice?"

"Something like that. Thomas will see
me in twenty minutes or so. Just thought
you'd like to know I was OK."

Roy revved the engine.
He was eager to be off.
But part of him was glad to know she was
all right.

"OK," he said.
Then he added, "Good luck. Don't expect
too much."

"Thanks," she said. "Thanks…"
She didn't seem to know what else to say.
She turned away and hurried back to the
house.

He watched her go.
Then he drove off.
He would have something to tell Susan
– and Jan – when he got back.

5

A call for help

He told them all the whole story when he got home.
Susan didn't know what to make of it.
She didn't want Roy picking up hitch-hikers.
Especially young girls.
But he wouldn't be told.

He almost got angry again, like the old Roy.
But he soon calmed down.
And Susan was secretly pleased he'd taken an interest in the girl.
In the past he had been so locked in his own world when he was driving, that no one else had mattered.

That could have been the end of it.
But it wasn't.

Roy was sitting at home one evening
when his phone rang.
Susan sighed.
It usually meant extra work – though she
didn't complain.
Any extra money was always welcome.
Jan hovered in the doorway.

He looked at his phone.
The caller was Chloe.
The girl.
He'd forgotten she had his number.

"It's Chloe Hammond," said the voice.
"I'm sorry to disturb you."

"Bloody hell," he said. "What on earth do
you want?"

"I'm sorry. I shouldn't have…"

"All right, all right. Just tell me."

"I saw Thomas. The faith healer. He asked lots of questions. He was kind and all that. But – I've got to take Dad there. For Thomas to heal him, I mean. And I don't know how to. We can't fit the wheelchair in our car and we can't afford a taxi all that way… Besides, I can't lift Dad into a car. I don't know – I just wondered if you were going that way again sometime. It doesn't matter when. Now I've said it, it's too much, isn't it? I'm sorry. I shouldn't have called."

"Shh!" said Roy. "Let me think. What does your dad think?"

"He doesn't mind. He doesn't care one way or the other really. Truth is, he's given up, so it's all the same whether he goes or stays at home. But he said he'd do it, if it pleased me."

"And your mum?"

"She thinks I'm mad. But she wouldn't stop me."

'I bet she wouldn't,' thought Roy.
"I'll think about it and call you back," he said. "Where do you live?"

"Bressenden. It's on the way to… "

"I know it," he said. "Speak to you later."

He told Susan.
She rolled her eyes to the ceiling.
"Once you get involved," she said, "you never know where it'll end."

"You think I shouldn't?"

She made a face and shrugged.
It meant: it's up to you.
In fact, she was amazed he was even
thinking about it.
But she wasn't going to start an
argument.
She preferred Roy the way he was now.
Gentler.
More caring.

"You going to take him?" asked Jan.

"I don't know. I might. Poor bloke. I can
imagine what it's like…"

Roy gazed out of the window, as if he
could see Chloe's father there.

"Go on, Dad! What have you got to lose?"

"Nothing, I suppose. If I'm going that
way. That's not the problem, though."

"What is?" asked Jan.

Roy turned away from the window.

"I don't want to see her face when she realises that her dad hasn't been cured."

That was the truth.
He could imagine the sick feeling –
knowing you were fated never to walk again.
That your last chance had gone.

But in the end he called Chloe back and he agreed to take her and her dad.
He would let her know as soon as he had a delivery to make that took him near Rudston.

It happened sooner than he had expected.

6

Errand of mercy

He stopped the lorry as close to number 32 as he could.

When he got to the door, it was already open.

Chloe stood there, much as he remembered her.

She introduced him to her father.

He, too, was dark haired – and had been handsome.

He had a careworn look and his smile was brief.

"Good of you," he said. "In fact, very good of you. I was cross when Chloe told me what she'd done. You've already helped a lot."

He stopped and shook his head.
He seemed to run out of energy.

Chloe pushed the wheelchair to the lorry.

"This is the tricky bit," said Roy. "Chloe,
you get in first. You can help your dad in.
I'm going to lift him up to you."

She did as he asked.
Roy hoped the man wouldn't mind being
lifted like a baby.
He was used to lifting heavy things – but
a person was another matter.

But it was easy.
The man used his arms to help pull
himself into the cab.

Roy folded the wheelchair and put it in
the back of the truck.
He got into the cab next to Chloe.
He leant over to her father.

"Roy Macmillan," he said.

The man took his hand.

"Jim," he said. "Pleased to meet you."

They set off.

Roy was glad that Chloe was next to him.

He didn't want to have to make
conversation with Jim.

It would be hard going.

As it was, it was OK saying the odd word
to Chloe.

She and her dad exchanged a few
comments.

The rest of the time they drove in silence
– a silence covered up by the regular roar
of the diesel engine.

Roy had planned the route carefully.

He did not want to drive through
Marston.

He did not want to drive past the accident
black spot.

He wondered if they had thought or
spoken about this.

He could not drive past the site of his own accident without a strange, sick feeling.
And he was a lorry driver.

Perhaps Jim blamed all lorry drivers for what happened.
It would be a natural reaction – to think all truckers were dangerous.
Roy looked in his mirror.
Actually, Chloe's father had closed his eyes.
He appeared to be sleeping.
Maybe the rhythm of the engine eased the pain.

Roy took the opportunity to speak to Chloe.

"What did your mum say when you phoned her from the Healing Centre?" he asked.

"She didn't know what to make of it," said Chloe. "She thought I was mad but she didn't really tell me off. She made me promise never to go off anywhere again, though. Without telling her, I mean."

"Did she want to come on this trip? Instead of you?"

"Not really. She doesn't reckon much to faith healers and stuff like that."

"And your dad?"

Roy said this quietly, half-glancing at the sleeping man.

"What about him?" asked Chloe.

"Does he reckon much to them?"

"Oh. Not really. I think he agreed just to please me. I was a bit surprised. I thought he would go into one of his moods."

Roy nodded.
He knew all about moods.

"Sometimes he hardly speaks for days," Chloe continued.

"That must be hard," said Roy.

"He never used to be like that," she said.

They fell silent for the next few miles. Roy pulled out some peppermints and offered her one.

Suddenly she spoke again.

"Thing is… he's angry," she said. She spoke just loudly enough for Roy to hear.

"He doesn't look angry."

"No. But underneath, he is. He's angry and he wants to blame someone. I suppose that's why he's so frustrated. He can blame the roads. He can blame the other drivers. And he blames himself for bad driving. He thought he was such a good driver."

She sounded like she was repeating other people's words.
Perhaps this is what her mother said.

"But most of all he blames life. Life has let him down."

'She's talking a lot,' thought Roy. 'That must be good.'

"Yes," he said. "So, he's, like, in some kind of sulk?"

She turned to him.
She gave him a smile and a frown at the same time.
"Yeah. That's it. That's exactly it!"

"I know all about that, too" said Roy, mainly to himself.

7

Waiting for a miracle

They reached Rudston by midday.
Chloe's father woke up just before they arrived.
Roy drove down the same lane and stopped by the entrance.
He got the wheelchair out and lifted Jim into it.
Chloe thanked him and pushed the chair towards the house.
"See you about four," she said. "And thanks," she added, almost as an afterthought.

"He could push his own chair," Roy muttered to himself. "It would be good for him. Why does he let her do it?"

Chloe turned and waved as they went
behind the corner of the building.
It was hard to drive off.

He drove steadily towards his destination.
He was in good time.
After he had made the delivery he stopped
at a service station and had something
to eat.
He hardly tasted it.
He didn't feel hungry – which was
strange.
He always felt hungry when he was
driving!

In an hour or so he would be back at the
Healing Centre.

Did he really expect to see Chloe and her
dad walking out together – pushing an
empty wheelchair?
Did she expect that?
And what did her dad expect?
Didn't faith healing depend on the faith of
the one being healed?

He shook his head.
He really didn't know – but he certainly cared.

It was overcast and rainy.
The truck squelched down the lane and into the stockyard.
It was the only place to turn round.
He backed up and swung the wheel.
A figure appeared at the gateway.
Roy wound down his window and leant out.
He didn't want to upset anyone – not today.
So he pretended it was his first time there.

He called down to the man at the gate.
"Rudston Manor Farm?"

"This is it. Not expecting any delivery," the man said, gruffly.

"Got a healing centre here?"

"You came past it. Back down the way you came in. On the left. Half a mile."

"Thanks."

Roy drove out of the yard and back down the lane.
He stopped by the gate.
No need to sound the horn.
If they were ready, they would be looking out for him.

Ten minutes went by.
Roy stopped smoking two years ago.
He ate another peppermint.
He turned on the radio and turned it off again.
The music got on his nerves.
The silly chat got on his nerves even more.
Another five minutes passed.

Then they came round the corner.

They looked no different.

Jim was in the wheelchair and Chloe was
walking behind.
The only difference was that her dad was
pushing himself along.

They reached the lorry.

"No instant cure!" said Jim, as soon as he
was close.

"Things take time," said Roy.
It was the safest thing to say.

He helped Jim up into the cab.

He turned to Chloe.
"I'll take care of the chair. Go and get in
the driver's side," he said. "Your dad will
have more room next to the door."
It was true.
But he really wanted to be able to talk to
her as they drove back.
And she might need to talk to him.

"How was it?" he asked as they hit the by-pass.

"I didn't stay with him," she said. "But I know what happens, sort of…"

She was quiet for a long while.
Then she said, "I know what you're thinking. 'He's still in the wheelchair. He still can't walk. It's all a con.'"

"Two out of three," he said.
He saw that her dad had closed his eyes again.
"How does he seem?" he asked.

"All right. I thought he might be really down – not being able to walk out of there. But he didn't seem to be. He was almost cheerful. Maybe, like, putting on a good show."

'Like you are,' thought Roy.
But he was relieved.

Driving two sad, depressed people back to Bressenden was what he had feared. So far, his fears had not come true – and soon it would be none of his business.

But then, that's what he'd thought last time.

8

Back to reality

Susan was out when he got back.
Jan was in the kitchen ironing some
clothes.
"How did it go?" she asked.

"No miracles," he said.

"Do you believe in miracles, Dad?"

"No," he said.

She went and filled the kettle.
"You look tired out," she said.
Since the accident she had taken to
worrying about him even more.
"What happened?"

"He came out in a wheelchair just like he went in – but they both seemed kind of…"
He searched for the word.
"… cheerful."
He didn't quite mean that.
"Cheerful is a bit of an exaggeration, but never mind."

"Is this guy a con artist, do you think?" she asked.

"Thomas Healing-hands? I don't know."

"She – what's she called?"

"Chloe."

"She seems a bit easily taken in."
Jan looked scornful.
As if she'd never be conned.
"Reads about this guy in the paper and, like, sets off to give him all her life savings!"

Roy frowned.

"Her life savings weren't that much! I don't think he charged a fortune. And her dad will be getting some compensation. I'm sure he'll pay her back."

He paused.

"She's a funny mixture. Soft but quite determined."

Jan made some tea.
She handed her dad a cup.

"It was the Internet," he said, taking a sip.
"Where she found out about him,
I mean."

"Even worse! You come across some right weirdos on that!"
Jan stood with her hands on her hips.

He could tell she thought Chloe was daft.
"In that case, she didn't do too badly. She might have ended up contacting some alien body clinic in the Highlands. Then I'd have been gone for weeks!"

Jan grinned.

She made a point of smiling at her dad's jokes.

It was nice that he made jokes again.

Before the accident he was so pressurised, so stressed, they never laughed together.

Jan became more serious.

"What if they ask you again? For help, I mean."

"Enough is enough. And I'll say so."

9

Out of the blue

Roy was driving when his phone beeped.
He stopped at the next lay-by.
It was a text message.

THANX!!! U R A * CHLOE

That was all it said.

He sat and thought.
It was three weeks since the trip to
Rudston.
Why would she thank him now?
Had her dad suddenly got up and
walked?
He was curious.

"Leave it," he said to himself.
But he couldn't.

He called her number.
It was answered straight away.
She sounded as if she was in a shopping mall.
"Yeah? Oh, yeah, hi!"

He had a picture in his mind of the three of them out shopping together.
He imagined the dad in the middle leaning on his wife and his daughter
– but walking.

"Just got your message. Why the sudden thank you? Is your dad…?"
He stopped at saying the word 'cured'.

"He's still in the wheelchair…" Chloe said. "He's not better. What I mean is, he's not cured. But he is better."

"What do you mean?"
Roy felt himself getting irritable.
Why did teenagers have to talk in riddles?

"He's just back to his old self. He's not depressed and miserable. In fact, we've just come back from the photographer's. I'm outside the place now. Mum and Dad are inside, paying."

"The photographer's?"
Roy didn't understand.

"Yeah. It was Dad's idea. Wanted a decent picture of us all together. First thing to spend some of his compensation on."

"Is that what's cheered him up?" asked Roy.

"No. He was different as soon as we got back from the trip. Well, as soon as he recovered. He slept for about twelve hours."

"Slept? He'd already slept in the cab. He must have been exhausted."

"It was nothing out of the ordinary. He just seems to have changed back to the person he used to be. Or more so. First, he thanked me for what I'd done. Couldn't believe what I'd done for him. And he sent me out to buy flowers for Mum. She nearly fell over when she saw them."

"I can imagine," was all Roy could say.

"I just had to thank you too. So while they're in there, I thought I'd text you. 'Cos without you…"

She trailed off.

"That's OK," he said. "There's no need…"

But he felt good.
Better than he had for a long time.
Like he'd been touched by the faith healer, too.

* * * * *

The letter arrived at the lorry depot.
The envelope was addressed to Roy.
The clerk handed it to him.
"Fan mail," she said.
He opened it.

Inside was a single photo.
There were the three of them: Jim in the wheelchair, with Chloe and her mum on each side of him.
They looked pretty good, but Chloe looked different.
Her long black hair was shiny and sleek; she was smiling and she was beautiful.

Later, he showed it to Jan.

He had told her about the phone call.

"So," he said, "would you go to all that trouble for me?"

She hesitated.
Then she gave him a hug.
"I'd take you to an alien body clinic, Dad, any time!"